PICOLA BOOKS

DANGEROUS INDISCRETIONS

DANGEROUS

INDISCRETIONS

Published by Shelby Britt

Dangerous Indiscretions is a work of fiction. Names, characters, places and incidents are either products of the author's imagination or are used fictitiously. Any resemblance to actual persons, living or dead, business establishments, celebrities, events or locales is entirely coincidental.

ISBN: 978-0692558492 (Shelby Britt)
Printed in the United States of America

OTHER TITLES BY PICOLA

Lies From His Heart
Available at amazon.com and barnesandnoble.com in
paperback and for Nook and Kindle users

Acknowledgments

Thank you for taking this personal literary journey with me. It amazes me that I was able to get up every day and create a piece of work that I can be proud of. For me, writing is not about getting recognition; it's about my personal journey and my passion. Thanks for taking this ride with me. It's going to be a great one.

To my baby Aaron: Yes, I know you are not a baby anymore, but I am so happy to have you in my life. You have been there through the ups and downs and I am glad that we are smiling again. It's getting better and better, son. I love you.

To my co-workers: Thanks for your eyes. Each one of you gave me great advice and let me know how you felt as I passed on pages of work for to you to critique. I really appreciate it from the bottom of my heart!

To my Lord and Savior: You have brought me from a mighty long way. There were and still are so many tears, sleepless nights and stressful days. But God, I'm still here!

Andrea

"Shit!" The pain shot from my neck straight to my forehead when I saw his number. I thought I was about to pass out as my cell phone vibrated and stopped me dead in my tracks. My ex-husband's name—Jason—flashed across the screen as I tried to comprehend what was happening. "Why in the hell is he texting me?" I hadn't heard from him since I filed for divorce four years ago.

Hey there, just wanted to say I miss you. Hope I'm not bothering you.

I took a hard breath and let out a nervous laugh. "Is he for real?" I sat at the kitchen table and stared at my phone. I didn't know what to do. My stomach was in knots. I had lost so much during my marriage to Jason, and after slowly getting back on my feet, here he was popping up out of nowhere.

The pain moved from my forehead to my right temple and throbbed. I closed my eyes and tried to figure out my next move. Should I text him back? Did I even want to re-live what he did to me? Where was he? Did he have a job? My mind played Jeopardy, and my phone vibrated again, waiting for a response.

"I'll take what is deleting the message for $600, Alex."

It was five o'clock in the morning, and I was up studying before work. I shook my head in disbelief. Frustrated, I closed my notebook and stared at the wall. If I had known about my ex-husband's financial problems while we were dating, I would have never married him.

Problems with the IRS and years of paying bills late tore our marriage apart. We were evicted out of two homes, foreclosed on another, and had multiple cars repossessed. We didn't have a chance. The day he walked out on me, Jason left a twenty-five-hundred-dollar mortgage, two car payments, and twenty thousand dollars in credit card debt. I was so naive. While I was out spending money lavishly, he was at home hiding the fact that he couldn't afford to pay our bills. He knew we didn't have a pot to piss in and decided not to tell me.

After our separation, I struggled to make ends meet. My job working as a wedding consultant for a bridal store hardly paid the bills, and I avoided the mailbox every chance I got because the only thing it held was bills. I swear, every time I opened a letter, it said "Your bill is past due, so don't let us catch your ass in the street."

Good thing my father and mother was able to support me financially until I could get things caught up. They gave me money each month to pay my mortgage and a little to help with the utilities. I was embarrassed having to ask another adult for money when I knew I was capable of doing it myself. They never questioned me, but even that train was slowly leaving the track, and I knew they wouldn't help me forever. I was free from the stress of my lying ex-husband and his financial woes, but I was still up to my eyeballs in the prison called debt.

Meanwhile, I kept myself busy. I met up with a new debt called financial aid and started online classes at the local university to get my master's degree in sociology. I started working out every night before bed to get my weight under control and hung out with my friends as much as possible. During that time, I even fell head over heels for a new man. With all the opportunities that were blossoming in my new single life, I was still unhappy. At night, I cried myself to sleep. But from nine-to-five, I put up a front so no one would know that everything in my world had crumbled.

For the most part, I was a strong woman, but today was one of those days. It was the kind of day when you open up another bill, and it's more than the balance of your bank account. The kind of day when I look down at my phone and realize my ex-husband had returned from the dead just as my new man lay in my bed.

Down the hall, Anthony's chocolate covered body lay still in the bed. His erection was up and ready for attention. Just four hours ago, my skin was ablaze as our bodies became one. I'd never been with someone who made me cum so hard, so often. The soft aroma of his Gucci Black cologne made me purr and tell him all my secrets whenever he was next to me.

At first, I smiled as I stared at him. A warm sensation ran through my body as I thought about how happy he made me feel. He was so protective of me and so loving that I didn't want to hide anything from him.

Anthony and I met in high school twenty-five years ago. I was the shy skinny girl who was in the drama club, and he was a rising high school football star. Anthony had since graduated from college and had become a well-known personal trainer with several DVDs and a book deal in the works. It was a breath of fresh air to find a man who was able to take me out to dinner without me paying the check.

On the inside, he was soft as a teddy bear, but on the outside, even his bright smile was overpowered by his dark skin and bulging muscles. His chiseled features drew attention from everyone when we were out together. I grinned, pretending I was with Dwayne Johnson while holding on to his large arms. His six feet two inches tall frame towered over my five-foot-two body. His arms were mounds of muscle, and I loved every bit of him.

Not long after my divorce was final, I started dating Anthony. Within six months, I became increasingly aware that Anthony had a bad temper. It seemed the smallest issue would ignite a fiery rage. Although it was never directed at me, deep down I hoped it would eventually go away, so I ignored it. Hell, I had been through worse with my ex, so I knew I could definitely handle something as minor as an occasional bad temper.

"What he doesn't know won't hurt us," I said, quickly deleting the message from Jason and climbing into bed next to Anthony. Guilt took over my mind like a dark cloud after I made the decision to keep the message I received a secret. I reached my hand over and softly trace the tattoos on Anthony's chest with my fingers as I waited for peace to return. My eyes traveled up and down the mountains of muscles in his arm as he stretched and yawned. His eyelashes fluttered as he focused on my face.

"Hey Sexy."

"Ready to go again?" he asked.

"You are too much," I replied with a teasing smile.

I gazed into his light brown eyes, and soon I was in a trance. I climbed on top of him, and my senses focused on him. His kisses were intense as the sunlight peeked its way through the blinds.

"We have to get ready for work," I whispered.

He sucked my tongue harder. "Just a bit longer, ok?"

"Yes, Oh, Oh, Oh yeah."

I moaned and ran my hands through my hair as I tried to keep up with his motions. He took me in and out of consciousness as we fell into a rhythm. He started to lose his breath as he tensed up and came. As he trembled, I lay on his chest, sweat dripping between us. My phone, laying on the nightstand next to the bed, vibrated again. I ignored it and held him tighter, hoping he didn't hear it. It vibrated again as I kissed him on his lips.

"You not gonna answer that?" he said, looking toward the phone.

I turned over and pulled the covers over our sweaty bodies. I glanced at the phone and saw Jason's name flashing across the screen.

"What the hell?" I mouthed to myself. Time stood still as I pondered what to say.

"Who is it, babe?" Anthony asked, turning to face me.

"Nobody, just work. They can wait," I said nervously.

"Ok, I'm getting in the shower." Anthony jumped out the bed. My eyes followed the outline of his naked body as the vibrating continued.

Butterflies danced in my stomach as I nervously watched the bathroom door. If Anthony knew that Jason had text me, let alone called me, he would flip.

Anthony's ex-wife cheated on him years ago. After a painful divorce, he was left angry and scared with trust issues. Although he was able to get past the hurt, he made sure that no one would ever cheat on him again by watching his new girlfriend closely.

He got angry and yelled at me when someone on social network would like my status. He would check my phone when I walked away to see whom I was texting. He hated to be *that* type of man, but he had to be cautious and sometimes took his anger out on anything and everyone around him. He was not going to allow himself to be cheated on again.

"I'm not worried about you," he would say with his fists balled up. "I'm worried about the men who don't care that you are with me. I will break their necks if they try to talk to you behind my back."

I made every effort to show him he didn't have to worry about any man taking my attention, especially my ex-husband.

Anthony was not fond of Jason. In fact, he hated him with a passion. And I saw his anger building up when I told him the story of my failed four-year marriage. He was visibly shaken when I cried about Jason not paying the mortgage, causing us to lose three of our homes. He balled his fist tightly as he watched my aggravation of discovering my wedding rings had been pawned because he needed the money to pay a bill.

"Anyone who would lie to his wife as much as he did isn't a man. I don't know what I'd do if I ever saw him, and I don't ever want to hear about him contacting you!" His words were matter of fact. I didn't think I would ever hear from Jason again. But then again, I didn't think it would ever snow in California.

As soon as the bathroom door closed behind Anthony, I rushed to pick up the phone. Clearing my throat and taking a deep breath, I spoke quietly into the phone. I had my left eye on the bathroom door as my left ear listened to the sounds of water splashing in the bathroom. My right ear pressed tightly against the cell phone as my breathing increased.

At any moment, Anthony could walk out of the room and realize I was talking to another man.

"Hello?" I whispered.

"Hey you." His tone was deep and soothing.

The beat of my heart thumped inside my ears as spoke.

"And you are calling me why?"

"I'm sorry, if I'm bothering you, I...I just wanted to say hi." His voice breezed through the phone softly. "I miss you."

My eyes widened. I tried to find the words, but I couldn't speak and I was in shock. I was so distracted by his words that I didn't hear the sounds of the faucet shutting off inside the bathroom. I tried to gather my thoughts, but they were all over the place. And at any moment, Anthony could walk back into the bedroom.

What just happened? Why is he doing this now?

Time was not on my side. I kept looking back at the door. My mouth was dry. I gulped and tried to swallow. I had to get him off the phone before Anthony walked out.

"Miss me? Are you serious?"

He chuckled at the sound of my confused voice. "Yes, is that wrong?"

My neck swung around at the sound of Anthony's toothbrush clicking on the sink. I looked around like I was hiding from the police.

"Look, I know I messed up, but we need to talk about a few things. I still love you." His words echoed in my mind.

Just as I was about to reply, Anthony opened the door. I quickly pressed the end button and threw the phone under my pillow.

With a white towel wrapped around his waist, Anthony stood at the door staring at me. Hanging my head down, I picked at my fresh manicure and held my breath.

Did he hear me talking? Please, please, please, don't let him realize what just happened."

With a straight face, Anthony walked over and stood in front of me. Water slid down his chest and landed on his legs. My body became weak as I waited for him to tell me what he had just heard.

The sides of his mouth curled into a grin as his towel dropped to the floor.

"Round three." He smiled, pushing me down on the bed, and kissed my neck. I inhaled deep from my lungs and rolled my eyes.

Thank you Lord. I had dodged my first bullet.

Jason

"Andrea, Andrea! Damn, she hung up on me." After hitting the steering wheel with his right fist, Jason adjusted his Gucci sunglasses and stared at his phone. "Maybe it's too soon, I shouldn't have called her."

It was the first of November and a mild sixty-five degrees. Sitting in the driveway of his three-story townhouse, Jason listened to the screeching sounds of the garage door slowly open. Putting the car in drive, he pulled his silver Cadillac ATS inside and turned off the engine. The garage door screeched again when it closed behind him.

Easing out of the car, he rubbed his hands across his chest, straightening his shirt. He checked his reflection in the window and smiled. There was a new man looking back at him. This was a man with confidence, a man who had a new lease on life. Jason closed his eyes and took a long, deep breath. He liked his new look but couldn't forget about his past. No matter what he did, he couldn't get her out of his mind. He took another long breath and stared at the ground.

Four years ago, Jason's life was turned upside down when he walked out on his wife, Andrea. Low paying jobs and problems with the IRS caused him to turn to drugs and alcohol abuse. Then the lies started. Too ashamed to tell her he couldn't afford to pay the mortgage, he hid the mail from her. When the foreclosure notices came, he started blaming his low hours at work. Before he knew it, they were being evicted.

The stress of having his third car repossessed caused him to drop from a healthy two hundred fifty pounds to a frail one hundred thirty-seven pounds. He used the bedroom as his hiding place. As he watched his marriage descend, he lost interest in himself and avoided his wife at all times. Hundreds of lies later, he sat home every night waiting for Andrea to come home and question why they were being evicted once again.

Blinking hard, Jason shook his head to forget the pain that haunted him for years and walked into the back of the house leading into the kitchen. The car keys clicked as he laid them on the all-white marble counter. Looking around the room, Jason stood in the kitchen, alone. The warm air from the custom floor vents moved up his pants legs and took the chill off his body. His lips curled into a devilish smile as his eyes moved past the expensive toys he purchased for his home. A fifty-inch flat screen TV hung on the wall in the kitchen, and in the great room a sixty-inch flat screen TV sat on the wall above the fireplace.

Jason stepped out of his black Stacy Adams, and walked over to the sofa and sat down. The soft black leather caressed his body, and he snuggled down to get relaxed. He picked up the remote lying next to him and pointed it at the box next to the fireplace. The soft sounds of a piano flowed through the surround sound speakers. Jason closed his eyes. He took a long, hard breath and held it for a moment. He exhaled like he was blowing out cigarette smoke. He thought about the holiday approaching. He was going to be alone again. Not only was it Thanksgiving, but the anniversary of his failed marriage.

Crossing his legs, he dug his feet deep into the fluffy white rug. It had been a rough four years without Andrea. After the separation, he ran away from North Carolina to Austin, Texas, and checked himself in a secret rehab facility. Months of sleepless nights and hours of counseling allowed him to kick the drug habit and realize it was he who caused the problems in his marriage. It wasn't Andrea not loving him, it wasn't losing his job; it was he who let himself down. When all the bills started to pile up, he shut down. He didn't know how to tell Andrea that he didn't have the money to pay them. He didn't want to look like a fool to her. He didn't want her family to know that he couldn't take care of his wife. It was like a nail was being hammered into his head slowly every day until he couldn't breathe anymore. Jason shut down mentally and emotionally. His bedroom became a hideout while the drugs became his escape. After getting clean, he decided to move on with his life and enroll in real estate school. With a new career on the horizon and clean from alcohol and drugs for almost a year, Jason filed Chapter 13 bankruptcy, borrowed money from his mother, and moved to Atlanta. He enrolled in real estate school and worked hard to become a well-known realtor to celebrities. He was living the good life.

He watched as the carpet moved between each toe as he surveyed the room and the new life he built. A new house he could afford, a new career, a fabulous car. What else could a man want? He rubbed his forehead slowly and took another long breath, this time blowing it out hard. Jason looked over at his phone sitting next to him and picked it up.

So many times he wanted to call Andrea and apologize for breaking her heart. So many times he wanted to pick up the phone and see if she was ok. Jason stood up and walked over to the silver safe hiding behind the island that separated the kitchen from the great room.

Reaching in, he pulled out a stack of papers and rubbed his fingers across the round seal on the front. Over and over he traced the letters on each page with his fingertips. With each touch, confirmation of his divorce was like a stab on each finger He slid down and sat on the floor next to the safe and closed his eyes. Sadness filled his body as he rocked back and forth.

"How could I let this happen?" he mumbled.

When the late notices started to come in from the bank, he hid them from Andrea. He tried to figure out a way to tell her that there was no money, but couldn't. Before he knew it, the car payment was past due two months. Thankfully, Andrea worked during the day, so he was able to hide all the late notices that came in. He knew she would find out eventually, and that time had come to an end and he knew his marriage was just about over. It was clear that she didn't want to see him again when the papers arrived at his mother's house. After all the lies he told her, she deserved to be free from him.

He bit his bottom lip, stood up and leaned against the counter. He thought of Andrea and her smile. He missed her laugh, her goofy dances and her soft kisses. He had hoped that maybe she missed him, too. But the way she hung up the phone when he called said something different.

It wouldn't hurt to call her again, he thought. Maybe she would forgive him. Scrolling through his contact list, he stopped on her name. He pushed the phone back into his pocket.

Sweat beads formed around his eyebrows as he became restless. Andrea was the only woman who really cared about him. She used to tell him that often when they were together, but he didn't listen. He had lost everything because of lies. Now he was divorced and living alone. He loved the life he was living, but all the fancy cars, invites to events with socialites, and selling millions of dollars in homes to celebrities couldn't hide the fact that his success was nothing without Andrea to share it with.

He thought about Andrea and the life he left her with when he walked out. She was probably eating peanut butter and jelly while he ate fresh salmon dinners. While he was flashing money to pay for new suits, she was probably going to the thrift store. He hated himself for allowing her to struggle.

"I've got to make this right. I've got to apologize and get her back," he said, throwing the white envelope back into the safe.

His mind was racing as he tried to gather his thoughts. It had been so long since he'd seen her, who knows what her life might look like. Was she with another man? Was she happy without him?

Maybe she's moved on with another man, he thought. *She sounded different when I called her earlier.*

He couldn't imagine seeing her with someone else. He paced in the kitchen. Every time he thought about Andrea, bad memories rushed through his mind. He stopped walking and glanced at the mirror next to the stairway. His reflection looked right into his eyes.

He swallowed and looked away. His breathing intensified at the thought of another man kissing Andrea. He looked back into the mirror and saw Andrea's soft caramel skin being caressed by a strange man's hands. His eyes widened as he heard the sounds of her voice purring as he watched the man's fingers touch her stomach. She turned her head and looked back into the mirror.

Pleasure and excitement showed on her face as she smiled and moaned softly. Just then, Andrea turned her head toward the mirror and smiled. The brown in her eyes rolled up as she put her head down and covered the strange man's penis. Jason's breathing became erratic; he hyperventilated. When she was done, she looked back into the mirror, locked eyes with Jason, and flashed a devilish smile.

Everything went black. Before he knew it, Jason had reached out and punched the mirror, shattering glass everywhere. His chest rose up and down as blood dripped from his right knuckles onto the dark brown marble tile.

"What the hell is wrong with me!" he yelled, holding his bloody hand up to his chest. His breathing staggered like a lion as he tipped around the pieces of glass and walked into the bathroom. Blood still dripping, he turned on the water and allowed the cold water to sooth his wounds. His breathing slowed as he looked up at the mirror over his head. His eyes were dark, and his face was sweaty.

He took a long hard breath and blew it out slow. He was tired. He wanted to be with her again. With his hand wrapped with a towel, Jason walked out of the bathroom and stood at the entryway to the hallway. Two of the bedroom doors were open, but one was closed. His hand tingled with pain as he held the tightly wrapped tourniquet he made out of the white terry cloth towel.

He hesitated as he took a few steps toward the closed door and stood in front of it. He took a deep breath and blew it out hard and turned the doorknob. The door made a cracking sound like a haunted house that hadn't been visited in some time. He was nervous as he stuck his head in and peeped around.

The room was empty except for a few brown boxes and large blue totes. The soft smell of jasmine filled his lungs as he closed his eyes. Jasmine was Andrea's favorite scent, so he made sure all the rooms had a candle with the same scent in each corner to remind him of her sweet smell.

White linen curtains swayed from side to side as the warm air flowed from the vents. Andrea didn't know where he was after the separation, so she took everything that was left in their house and had it shipped to his mother's house. He turned on the light and kneeled down in front of biggest tote. The lid was covered with gray masking tape except for a small white square that had the words "our wedding way" written on it.

This was the only box that Jason hadn't opened since moving in to his townhouse. He knew those words meant two things. Either it was stuff from their wedding or it was stuff from her job and she sent it by mistake. He hoped it was from her job. Just the thought of her sending something from their wedding day made his heart ache.

Just as he was about to open the lid, the phone inside his pocket started to vibrate. He ignored the tingling of pain that was moving through his right hand as he struggled to reach into his right pocket with his left hand. Just as he pulled the phone out, the vibrating stopped.

He gasped with shock as he stared at the name flashing across the screen. Andrea's name was next to the words "missed call."

"Wow, she called." His lips curled up into a smile. "Maybe this is the confirmation I need to get my wife back."

Anthony

I've been told that I'm one of the nicest assholes you would ever meet. It's a true statement, and I'm arrogant as hell. That's just how I am, so people need to take it or leave it. When I was younger, I was teased because of my dark complexion and small frame. I was called JJ from *Good Times* so many times I started to believe I was really him. The more people teased me, the worse my arrogance grew over the years.

The one thing that has been consistent is women. I love them, and they love to hate me. I'm afraid of being hurt. I've always competed with light-skinned brothers, but right now dark meat is in, so I'm taking advantage of it while I can.

I consider myself a good catch. After graduating college, I lived at the gym and studied weight training. I received my personal training certification and released a workout video called *Work Your Abs.* I have a decent life, but I also have a few issues.

My ex-wife of three years cheated on me with another man, which has caused my heart to harden. After the divorce, I took on the "I don't give a shit what anyone thinks" attitude. Some people call it a short fuse, but I call it having a deep hate for people who don't take care of their responsibilities. That pisses me off.

When I started dating Andrea, she told me about her scumbag of an ex-husband and how he left her with piles of debt. I vowed to make sure she wouldn't hurt again and treated her like a queen. We were the perfect couple and because we were both divorced and had unreliable exes, we leaned on each other for support.

Although I knew Andrea would never cheat on me, my trust issues and bad temper would always get in the way and make me suspicious of her actions. When we're together and she receives a text message from someone, thoughts run through my mind and I wonder if she is cheating. If she was talking to someone on the phone, and I walked in the room, I would question her about who she was talking to until I felt she wasn't telling a lie.

I know Andrea is different and truly loves me, but I choose to keep my guard up at all times just in case something happens. I don't want to be this way, but it is what it is, and I can't do anything about it. Once I sense something's not right, no one has a chance with my temper or my attitude. And thanks to my cheating ex-wife, I've been given a life sentence of not trusting people.

I remember the day that ended our marriage. Janet, my wife, was in the kitchen cooking dinner. I had just come home from work and walked upstairs to our bedroom to change my clothes. I remember seeing her cell phone lying on the bed as I took my shirt off. I glanced at the screen and saw the words missed call. Three minutes later, the phone started to vibrate and vibrate and vibrate.

It wasn't unusual for Janet to leave her phone lying around. In fact, we both sometimes answered each other's calls. We didn't have secrets, I thought, and I was a loyal husband. When the vibrating started to get out of control, I had to pick it up.

"Who in the hell keeps texting her?" Irritated at the constant vibrating, I grabbed the phone and pushed the button on the side to shut it off. Just as I was about to sit the phone back down on the bed, my eyes moved across four words that halted my breathing: *Hi sexy, it's Johnny.*

My vision became blurry. I wiped my eyes to make sure I was reading those words correctly. I wanted to throw the phone against the wall. But I didn't. Instead, I kept reading messages from "Mr. Johnny."

7:10 p.m.: Hey sexy, can't wait to see you again.

7:15 p.m.: Hey good looking, I miss those soft lips of yours, call me soon.

7:20 p.m.: Can't wait to hold you in my arms again

7:25 p.m. Hey sweet-face I'll meet you at noon.

One by one, the words slapped me in my face and pierced my heart. I dropped my head and closed my eyes. The same woman who vowed to love me forever was now vowing with another man. Sweat started to form on my forehead as I stared at the phone.

The aroma of seasoned steak and mashed potatoes made its way through the air vents above my head and filled my chest. I ignored the sounds moving around in my stomach that reminded me that I hadn't eaten yet.

My body was numb and my feet were cement. I sat on the side of the bed staring at the wall. A wave of emotions moved through my body like a tornado. Sadness caused tears to form and linger around my eyelids. "I've been so good to her, how could she do this to me."

Confusion danced around in my head. "Where did she meet him? What did I do to deserve this?" Finally, rage shoved its ugly head through my chest and caused it to tighten like a rubber band. "I am going to kill her!"

Pain was in my face as I pushed myself off the bed. Janet was standing at the bedroom door with a look of horror on her face as the tears dropped from my eyes. The look of her made my skin crawl, and the rage inside of me took over like a demon.

"Who the fuck is this dude, and why is he texting my wife?" I yelled.

She froze and tried to open her mouth to talk but nothing came out. Fear in her eyes intensified as she listened to me read aloud the messages that "Mr. Johnny" had sent to her earlier that day.

My breathing was heavy and my chest rose up and down as my anger grew stronger. My hands were shaking. I stood up and walked toward her.

"Bitch, you must be crazy to cheat on me! I'm gonna kick somebody's ass!"

Janet's back pressed against the bedroom door as she took a step back. I saw Janet's panic as I rushed her.

I needed her to hear me loud and clear. Aggravation filled my lungs as I screamed out the words to her, loud and slow, "I'm going to ask you again, who is Johnny?" I yelled so hard that her body flinched. Her eyes danced with fear and her voice trembled.

"Just let me explain, Anthony," she pleaded.

The sounds of Andrea singing louder took me out of my trance and back to reality. I squeezed my eyes tight and rubbed my temples hard. I didn't want to remember what I did that night to my ex-wife. I hated Janet for making me feel this way. She turned me into the "angry black man." If it wasn't for her stupid ass, I'd be able to love and trust a woman like a man is supposed to. That bitch made me trust no one.

For some odd reason, Andrea was not acting like herself. Normally a night of passionate love was enough for me to keep her attention on me, but this time was different. Something was off with her. The elephant was sitting in the room with us and it wasn't the stench of freshly made love either.

Maybe it was the way she jumped and threw her phone under the pillow when I walked into the room after taking a shower. Of course I saw it, but I didn't say anything to her.

I walked over and kissed her face. She smiled at me. I kissed her neck, and we both fell back on the bed. She let out a deep breath, and I felt her uneasiness against my chest. Something was wrong with her. Her body was tense and the sensation of power had left her body. I looked up at her eyes and grinned.

"I really have to get ready for work, baby," she said with a crooked smile. Hesitating, I pulled myself off her and sat up on the bed next to her. The comforter was damp from the shower.

"What's wrong, did I do something?"

She slid up to the edge of the bed, causing her white t-shirt to move just above her right thigh. Her shoulders weakened as she frowned and walked away and stood in front of the mirror that hung across the bedroom door. She moved a few stray hairs behind her ears as the reflection looked back at her.

"Of course not." She turned around and flashed me a reassuring grin. "I just have a lot of work to do today, and I don't want to be late." She walked back over to me and gently placed her hands around my neck. Softly kissing my forehead, she whispered in my ear, "You are all I have and all that I love."

She had me wrapped around her finger and my heart softened. I watched the silhouette of her body underneath the t-shirt prance across the room and disappear into the bathroom. Minutes later, soft humming sounds vibrated from underneath the door. I took a deep breath as my lungs filled with the scent of lavender. Whenever she took a bath, she used a lavender shower gel that filled the room. That smell aroused me and had me wanting her even more.

But as quick as I became aroused, something in the pit of my stomach started to ache. Something was off with her today. She never turned me away, even when she was tired.

Sitting there trying to figure out what was wrong with Andrea had caused me to forget I had to go to work. My alarm clock buzzed as I jumped up to turn it off.

"Damn, good thing I ironed my clothes last night." I rushed over to the closet and took my clothes off the hanger. The uneasiness in my stomach moved around like butterflies as I hurried to get dressed. I hated feeling like I couldn't trust people, especially Andrea

The sound of soapy water rushing down the drain moved through the vent over my head as I grabbed my wallet off the dresser and opened the bedroom door. I wanted to wait to kiss her goodbye, but my thoughts were all over the place.

Was Andrea hiding something from me? I looked at the bathroom door, shook my head, and walked out of the room. As I walked out of the house to my car, I took another deep breath, this time holding it in. I knew eventually I'd find out what she was hiding. At some point everything that is done in the dark will come to light.

I stepped in the car and closed the door. As the engine revved up and down, I mumbled, "If I find out that she is cheating on me, life will be hell for her…and him.

Andrea

The hot water beat down on my face as I stood in the shower. I stood there naked with my head down and my eyes closed. Taking deeps breaths, the steam filled my lungs and I blew them out slow. I leaned against the wall with both my hands pressed against the silver and gray tile like I was under arrest. My eyes were closed and my thoughts were running down the drain with the water. Butterflies filled the pit of my stomach, and I was sick with nervousness. I wanted to get that voice out of my head. I tried so hard to forget about Jason and the financial issues we had when we were married, but I was curious as to what he wanted after all this time.

"I have got to shake this feeling off," I mumbled. I knew this feeling all too well. The butterflies and I had become best friends. Years ago when Jason was often late paying the house note, I became afraid to walk to the mailbox. My legs wobbled and the coldness of fear rose up and down my spine as I took small steps toward the black box. Opening the lid seemed to take hours as I looked at the white envelopes sitting inside waiting for me to pick them up. My heart beat a mile a minute as the words LATE NOTICE became permanently embedded in my mind.

Those words were like the plague that jumped inside my body and attacked all of my organs, causing me to shut down. The thought of seeing an eviction notice or a foreclosure letter was like an inmate waiting on death row. You know it's coming; you just don't know when. So you wait and wait and wait.

There were no eviction notices to be read this time. But the remnants of an old situation had started to lurk around. My old friends, the butterflies, had begun to fill the pit of my insides and start their dance.

"Maybe humming will help me release this," I said, adjusting the shower head from full stream to light jets. Humming always made me feel better. Plus if I was too quiet in here, Anthony would think there was something wrong with me, and I didn't want him to know my ex-husband had just called me.

"I need to get out of this shower. I know Anthony is wondering what is going on." I let out a breath and shook my head. I wrapped the fuzzy green towel that sat on the edge of the sink around my body and walked over to the door. I stuck my head out the door and started to smile.

"Hey honey?" I hummed slow and soft. My eyes danced around searching for him, but the room was empty. I expected to see him sitting on the side of the bed, but he wasn't there. I held my towel tight against my chest as I walked past the closet and stood in front of the bedroom door. I frowned.

Why did he leave? I thought. *Is he mad at me? Why would he leave and not say anything to me?*

My mind filled with questions as I turned and started to get dressed.

OMG! I hope he didn't look at my cell phone. I started to panic and ran over to the side of the bed that I had slept in. I gulped and slid my hands under the pillow, searching for the phone. My fingertips felt it as I grabbed and exhaled hard. It was still there. "Damn! This is too much for one person to deal with." I ran over to the closet and grabbed a pair of black dress pants and a red t-shirt and dressed as if my life depended on it. I rushed down the stairs, grabbed my keys off the kitchen counter and ran out the house, slamming the door behind me. I jumped in the car and shoved the key into the ignition. I pressed my foot softly on the pedal and listened to the engine purr.

I looked down at my black leather Prada purse sitting next to me on the passenger seat. I was proud of that purse and carried it every day. It was a constant reminder of how my money used to flow before I got married.

The sunlight shifted and beamed down through the windshield and bounced off the chrome siding on my cell phone. The glare reflected into my eyes, and I squinted and scrambled to grab my sunglasses out of the glove box. I mumbled to myself as I rushed to get out of the driveway. "There is no way I can allow this man to stress me out again. I have come too far to do this all over again. I scrolled through the contact list and stopped on Jason's name. My thumb traced the outline of his name over and over as I pondered what to do next. "What the hell." I pressed the call button.

I needed to see what he wanted. I wanted to ask him where the hell did he get off calling me after all this time. Where the hell did he get off saying he missed me? Does he even realize the state of mind he left me in? Does he know the financial hardship I was dealing with?

Anger built inside my gut as I listened to the phone ring. I was about to hang up after the third ring when he picked up.

"Hello? Hey there." His voice was soft and upbeat. I couldn't find the words to speak. My mind went blank. Hearing his voice took me back to his last words to me, the last words he spoke as my husband: *I'll be back to get the rest of my stuff.*

"Andrea? Hello?" His voice trailed off in confusion.

"Umm, Hi Jason." I managed to get the words out in a whisper. My mind shot back to four years prior and thrust me into an emotional state that I didn't want to revisit.

"Hey, it's good to hear your voice again. I must have called you too early, huh?"

The anger that I released some time ago was returning, and I wanted to curse at him. But mentally, I was in a better place and had forgiven him for what was done. I shook my head and regained my composure.

"No, no. I was just in the middle of something. Look, why were you texting and calling me like that after all this time?"

My ear pressed tightly against the phone as I nervously waited for him to respond. As he cleared his throat and started to speak, his voice was deep and raspy. I could tell he was smoking again and that bothered me. Why I don't know.

"I was thinking about you, and I finally got the nerve to call you. I just wanted to apologize, and I just wanted to know that you are ok. Is that wrong of me?"

I paused. "I don't know what you want me to say, Jason. I wasn't expecting this."

"I'm sorry. I didn't mean to bother you. I'm sure it's a surprise to hear from me. I understand if you don't want to talk to me."

I looked at the clock on my dashboard and frowned. I was already running late for work as is and now I was really going to be late sitting here trying to figure out what he wanted.

My leg trembled. Even though my mind was all over the place, his voice relaxed me just like when we were married.

I swallowed and struggled to catch my breath. "No... It's too late now. What's done is done."

"Are you busy right now? I know that things were left rocky, but I still love you. I want to know that you are ok." He hesitated as he tried to get the words out. I took the phone off my ear and stared at it.

This was not happening. What in the world do I say back to him? My heart softened, and I almost forgot about the lies he used to tell me. When we were married, I questioned everything he said to me. But for some reason, this time, I believed him. I started to feel comfortable talking to him. It felt like old times when everything was ok and I could talk to him about anything.

"Are you seeing anyone new? he asked.

I swallowed again and looked out the window. Hesitating, I took a long breath. I couldn't answer. I wanted to scream out that I was in love with a wonderful man who didn't lie to me. But the words didn't come out. I wanted to squeal and tell him how my new man made me feel like a queen. But I didn't. Before I knew it, I quietly said, "I'm late for work. Can I call you later?"

"Sure you can. I'd like that. Talk to you later." His smile came through the phone.

"Bye." I put the phone down in my lap and lay my head on the steering wheel. I closed my eyes and exhaled.

"Why did I do that? Why didn't I just say I was dating again? Why didn't I tell him that?" My stomach had a weird feeling. I was nervous, scared and confused.

What did I just get myself into? Four years and I was finally able to be happy with someone else and trust again. Four years of struggling, trying to get out of debt and depending on my parents to help pay my bills. Four years of wondering if there was something wrong with me. All of that and I couldn't tell him to kiss my ass, go to hell or just not answer the phone.

"Damn it!" I yelled, looking at the clock on the dashboard. "Damn him! I'm late as hell for work!" I put the gear shift into reverse and pushed on the gas. Just as I was about to move the gear into drive, I heard a loud cracking sound. My right foot stomped on the breaks and I put the car in park. "No!" I screamed, looking out the rearview mirror. I backed the car into the tree stump that sat next to the driveway. I jumped out and walked to the back of the car. Pieces of wood were broken and sitting in the back of the tail light. Pieces of red glass were shattered on the cement next to the tire. I put my hands over my mouth and made a sound as I blew my breath out long and hard.

"This is not happening." I shook my head and walked with my head hung low back to the car and slumped myself in the driver's seat.

I rubbed my temples as tears started to roll down my right cheekbone. I didn't need any more bills. Hell, I didn't need any more issues in my life. Even though I had a little help, I was still in debt. I could barely keep my car payment up and now this happened. It was like bad luck hit me in my face every time that man was involved. The entire time I was married I had money issues or something came up that I didn't have the money for. And just like clockwork he called, and something dealing with money popped up.

I guess he thought he could just call me out of the blue and things would be ok. I guess he thought after four years I would have forgotten all he'd put me through.

"Lord Jesus," I whispered. "I can't catch a break." I grabbed my purse and walked back up the driveway and into the house, leaving the car door open so that it could get

to know the tree stump a little better.

Jason

Two weeks went by, and I couldn't get Andrea out of my head. The sound of her sweet voice was like a taste of heaven. When we were married, she stuck by my side and tried her best to assure me she loved me. But I messed that up by not communicating with her and telling lies about what I was doing with my money. Things have changed now, and I'm a better person. I just need her to see that.

The last time I talked to her, she said she would call me back, but she never did. I didn't want to pressure her, so I didn't call or text her. I wanted her to absorb what I said to her. I wanted her to know that what I said was the truth.

Waiting for Andrea to call me back was painful. Not knowing what she was thinking was killing me, and I didn't know what to do. I tried to keep busy by showing a few houses and updating new home listings online, but I couldn't concentrate.

I had to see her. I wanted her to know that we needed to be together again and that I could be a better man to her. I wanted to put my arms around her and apologize for each and every time she felt afraid. I wanted to tell her I was sorry for all that I put her through. I wanted to buy back everything that she lost when we moved from house to house. I had nothing to lose. I had already lost her one time, and I didn't want to lose her again. Things were better this time around, and I wanted to show her how good things could be. I was bringing in lots of money. I owned my own house, and I had a car. All I needed now was for her to complete me and be my wife again.

Time stood still as I sat in my car. I waited and waited for hours for her to come home. I kept looking at my watch and looking over my shoulder. I couldn't believe

I was doing this, but I did. I had the perfect view of the two-story white house with the white picket fence. I nervously adjusted the rearview mirror to make sure I had a good view of the street traffic. It was 6 p.m. and almost dusk. It was the time of the day when the birds start to move to their evening hideouts in the trees and the lighting bugs got ready to glow in the dark.

My anxiety intensified as neighbors walked by the car speaking in slang. It had been so long since I was here that I didn't want anyone to recognize me. But then again, I looked like a completely different person compared to how I used to look.

I sat low in my seat and adjusted my sunglasses. I needed to take the edge off while I waited, so I turned on the radio. I had no idea what time she would be coming home. I was here now, so it didn't matter. I had nothing but time. I lay my head back on the headrest as the soft sounds of Earth, Wind and Fire filled the car. They were our favorite group when we were married. No matter what the cost and no matter where in the country they were performing, Andrea made sure to purchase tickets for us to see them. I used to feel uncomfortable about her buying things for me when I couldn't afford them, but she did it anyway. That was Andrea's nature. She was caring and giving.

And that's why I'm sitting here, doors away from the house that we used to share. Sitting here like a thief in the night. I know I should have called first, but I had to see her. The last time I talked to her I didn't think about how she would react to me. I didn't think about how she would feel seeing me after all this time, but I had to take the chance. I sat here, waiting to get a glimpse of her. I couldn't wait to see her reaction when she saw my hands holding the dozen red roses I got for her. The huge hug and kiss she'd given me when she realized how much she had missed seeing me. I couldn't sit at home any longer and wait for her to call me back. That's why I was here.

As Philip Bailey hit a high note, my head nodded and my chin slowly touched my collarbone. I was tired. My eyes were heavy, and my breathing was slow as I floated in a deep nap.

Just as I was about to get into a zone with Philip Bailey's high notes, I was pulled away by the sound of a high-pitched horn. I jumped up and gripped the steering wheel. My knuckles turned white as I leaned forward and stuck my head out the window

"She's home!" I quickly put my head back in and looked out the rearview mirror. A red car was whizzing down the street, gliding in and out of traffic. I remember when we were married; I'd always tell her she had a lead foot and to slow down. Andrea loved driving fast.

I was excited like a kid on Christmas day as I pulled down the visor and wiped the sweat that formed around my forehead with the palm of my hand. I stared at my reflection in the mirror. My stomach made noises. I didn't eat anything because I was scared I would miss seeing her.

When we were married, Andrea worked the first shift at her job. It was almost seven in the evening so I was here at the right time. My stomach was in knots. I looked at myself again and made sure my eyebrow hairs weren't out of place.

I stroked my mustache and replayed what I was doing here. It happened so fast. I woke up this morning and packed a bag and drove all the way from Atlanta to Austin to see her. She didn't say she was seeing anyone when I asked her, so this was going to be a perfect meeting. I needed to see her soft brown face—that beautiful smile she had. I wanted to touch her soft skin. I was taking a chance, but it was a chance that had to be taken.

A red corvette with chrome rims crept down the street and pulled up in front of the house that we used to share four years ago.

"She must be doing really well," I said. She was driving an old beat up red Honda the last time I saw her. "I guess life is treating her good." I smiled.

The headlights turned down and the door opened. I unbuckled   my   seat   belt.   "She is going to be so surprised!" I put my hand on the door and pushed it opened.

My lips parted to call out her name, but my eyes had another plan. I looked down and a pair white of Adidas were placing themselves on the ground next to the car. Confused I eased back into the car and slowly closed the door. Pain ran between my eyes.

The man eased out and stood next to the car. He was about six foot two and dark as the street he stood on. He was clean shaven except for a very light mustache that framed his top lip. The white T-shirt he wore was hidden by all the muscles that protruded from underneath. Two sleeves of tattoos adorned each arm. I'd never stared at another man this long, but I was intrigued at who he was.

He closed the door behind him and took a look behind him. For a moment, we locked eyes, at least I thought we did. He pulled off his gold aviator sunglasses and looked harder. He was searching for something. His eyes were blinking as he tried to focus. I stared at him harder.

Sweat ran down the back of my neck. Is he looking at me? Did he know who I was? Who was this man? Maybe he is going into another house, I thought. I scrambled to figure out what to do next. Our eyes were glued to each other as my mind raced. I grabbed my phone and searched for her phone number. I held the phone to my ear, waiting for her to answer. I waited to hear her voice. I needed to hear her say she had moved to another house. I prayed that

I was at the wrong house. Maybe this guy was a long lost cousin I had never seen before. But whoever this man was, I had to find out.

I blew my breath hard as I listened to her voicemail. I hung up and dialed the number back. Why wasn't she answering me? Just as I heard the voicemail pick up again, Mr. Darkness, dressed in blue jean shorts that just touched his knee cap, reached into his back pocket and pulled out his cell phone. His red fitted baseball hat was turned to the side and a toothpick hung out of his dark lips. He was obviously under the age of forty.

My eyes were still on him as he flashed a wide smile. He gave a quick nod and showed all his white teeth. He waved his hand, signaling my way.

"Is he waving at me?" My face frowned in confusion. I adjusted my seat so I could get out and speak to him. "Maybe he does know who I am." I put my hand on the door to push it open when a deep scratchy voice rang out behind me.

"Hey now!" The voice behind me yelled. My head swung around and saw an older man in his 60s walking up to the house next to me. His dark brown pants and his green and white checkerboard shirt seemed to hang from his frail body as he waved at Mr. Darkness and sat down on the red concrete steps of his porch.

Smoke swirled around the old man's his head as he took a deep breath and inhaled quickly. His mouth puckered as he pulled the white cigarette from his lips and flicked it onto the ground. It bounced in the grass in front of him. My heart pushed through my chest as it beat a mile a minute. Grabbing a napkin, I wiped my face and cursed. I was mad at myself. "Man, shit! I thought he was looking right at me. I'm paranoid."

I eased back down into my seat and took another hard breath, this time holding it to calm my nerves.

Where in the hell is Andrea? I thought.

Frustrated, I rubbed my chin. "I need to find out who this dude is." My breathing was heavy as the air flowed in and out of my nose. Just as I was about to push myself out of the seat, a soft sound of laughter rang out. I looked up and saw her.

It was Andrea. She was walking out the big white house, smiling from ear to ear. She had on a white short-sleeve button down shirt that was tucked inside a red flowing wrap skirt. She seemed to glide down the walkway. She was beautiful. Her long brown hair bounced off her shoulders, falling back into place with every step she took.

She was glowing as she ran over to Mr. Darkness and kissed him on the lips. My heart dropped and I lost my breath. My mouth fell open as I watched her embrace him and lay her head on his chest. I leaned closer to the steering wheel and watched him squeeze her back gently and open the car door for her. He closed the door after her and returned to his side of the car and slid in. I fell back, hitting my head on the seat. Heartbroken, I had to leave. I reached my head up and started the ignition. So many questions ran through my head. I didn't know what to think. But at that moment, I knew three things. I had to get the hell outta here. I had to find out who Mr. Darkness is. And I had to talk to Andrea.

Putting my hands on the gear shift, I wondered if he even noticed me sitting in the car. Was it my imagination that he looked right into my eyes? There was no way he could not have seen me. If I were him, I would have walked over and said something.

I could have sworn he looked right at me. I shook my head and rubbed my fingers across my eyebrows. What the hell did I just do? Is that her new man? Who is he? Is she married? Is that her boyfriend? I had so many questions and no answers.

I became pissed. I drove all this way to see her for nothing. I pulled off from the curve and my tires screeched. Before I passed the little red corvette, I slowed down just enough to sit beside Mr. Darkness. The windows were dark. I could only see shadows. I stared long enough for someone to see me. Maybe *she* would notice me. I wanted her to get a glimpse of me. At this point, I didn't care what happened. I was playing with fire.

Just then, the shadow in the passenger seat looked over in my direction and locked eyes with me. She realized who I was and turned away fast. That's all I needed to see.

I pushed my feet down hard on the pedal, making my tires screech loud as I sped away, leaving smoke in the wind. Sweat ran down the side of my right temple. I balled my lips up in disgust.

"I need answers," I mumbled as I turned up the music. There was no way another man was going to take my wife away from me. I would get to the bottom of this if it was the last thing I do. She had my attention. And so did Mr. Darkness. That wasn't a good thing.

Andrea

What the hell? My body went cold. A chill ran through my neck and down to my fingertips. Air filled my lungs like a balloon as I looked over at the man sitting in the car next to us. I recognized his face. I looked right into his eyes. His eyes were dark and burned a hole right through the car window. I'd seen that look before. The same look my ex-husband had when I told him our marriage was over. The same look he had when he walked out the house and left my life in shambles.

The vents blew cool air that gently moved my hair off my forehead. I wiped my forehead. This was not real. Maybe the eighty-degree weather was getting to me. I had to be hallucinating.

Was that...Jason, I thought. No, there was no way. I heard from a friend that he lived in Atlanta. He wouldn't dare show up unannounced. I rubbed my eyes with my fingertips. I looked back up, and he was still there. He was staring at us.

Busy looking through which CD he wanted to listen to, Anthony hadn't noticed the gold Cadillac sitting next to him. As I looked over at Jason, the sides of his mouth curled up into a devilish grin. I turned my head quickly toward the house and made a gasping sound.

The shit was about to hit the fan.

"Did I leave the dog outside again?" I moved my head side to side as if I was looking for the dog in front of the house.

Anthony frowned. "Come on, man, it's time to go. You know what, I'll look real quick." He put the CDs down and shook his head in disappointment.

As his seat belt slapped against the tan leather seats, the gold Cadillac revved its engine and sped off, leaving a cloud of smoke next to the car.

"What the fuck!" Anthony yelled, jumping back. My mouth dropped as I looked through the smoke at the gold car disappearing into the evening dusk. "Who in the world was that?" His forehead wrinkled up as he looked at me.

I kept a surprised look on my face. My shoulders hunched up and my mouth opened wide. "I have no idea."

"Do you know that guy?" Anthony looked at me. Who was that, Andrea?" The veins in his neck popped out and his breathing was hard.

My tone was high soprano. "What are you talking about? I'm just as shocked as you." I looked down at my skirt and adjusted the pleats. I was nervous.

"Nobody does that, Andrea. Why would some random man just pull up beside the car and speed off like that unless he is trying to prove a point?"

I sat there in silence. I didn't know what else to say. I'd seen Anthony become angry before, but this was different. His eyes were squinting, and his tone was deep and sharp. He definitely not the soft teddy bear I normally saw. He wanted an answer, but I wasn't ready to give him one. The longer I stayed quiet, the angrier he became.

If I told him the man in the gold car was my ex-husband, he would chase him down and kill him. I was not going to allow that to happen.

I became aggravated. The silence was going on for too long. I just wanted to forget I even saw Jason. I wanted to forget what Jason had done to me.

"Can we just please go? You are making a big deal out of nothing." I crossed my arms and sucked my teeth.

"I don't even want to go now," he said, grabbing the wheel. The keys rattled as he turned the car off and put the car in park.

"What are you doing?" I yelled, confused.

I looked at him, but he turned his back to me and looked out the window. "I said I don't want to go anywhere!" He spat the words out to me like I was a stranger on the street. His face was tight, and his hands were gripping the steering wheel. "Just go back into the house and I'll talk to you later."

I couldn't figure out why he was mad at me. One day I'm trying to figure out why Jason's calling me. The next day, he's in front of my house stalking me. This tea was sweet like chocolate and my teeth were aching. And now Anthony was blaming me for something I had no control over.

So many things ran through my head. I should have told him the day Jason text me. I should have told him he called me. I pondered my thoughts. I wondered if Jason would be here if I would have just called him back weeks ago. But instead, I acted like I didn't care and didn't speak a word to Anthony.

A secret is a hell of a drug.

"What did I do? I didn't do anything!" I turned my body toward him. He didn't look at me. He turned his head and stared out the window. His chest rose up and down.

"Anthony? Anthony? I yelled. "Are you serious? Now you're not talking to me? You are a piece of work, man." Reaching down by my waist, I took off my seat belt and grabbed my purse. "Whatever, Anthony. I'm going inside." I slowly opened the door. Before I could get my second leg out, he started the car. With half of my body out of the car, I looked back at him. He looked straight ahead as if he was in the car alone.

"So you're just going to leave and not say anything to me?" I waited for a response, but he wouldn't give me one. I let out a long breath and stepped out of the car and closed the door. Before I could stand up straight, Bobby Brown was still humping around. Bending down to adjust my skirt, the warmth from the engine hit my face.

I held my breath and felt the air rush across my legs. Anthony put the car into drive and sped off, leaving me on the sidewalk. I looked up in shock. Did he really just leave like that? I didn't know what to do. I hoped no one was watching. Embarrassed, I stood in one place, scared to look around. My heart beat drowned out the faint sounds of someone quietly calling my name. But I didn't respond. I was scared to look up. The whisper became louder while I looked down at the ground. "Andrea...Andrea!"

I blinked hard and looked to my left. It was Anthony sitting next to me in the car. He had turned around and come back.

"What?" I exhaled hard. My hands shook like I needed a cigarette. I put my hands over my mouth and shook my head hard. "Oh my God!" I said to myself. "My mind is playing tricks on me." I had stood there so long I didn't hear him come back.

Blowing out a deep breath, Anthony shook his head. "Come on and get in the car! I'm hungry."

Did I just make up what just happened in my head? I was losing touch with reality. Had Jason's appearance caused me to go crazy?

"What is wrong with you, Andrea? Get it together," Anthony said, shaking his head. "I'm still mad. I just want to just go." Anger colored his face and made his dark skin even darker.

Where in the hell did Jason get off showing up without a phone call or a text? Was he stalking me? Why was he doing this to me? Was he trying to get back at me for divorcing him? Was he mad because I didn't call him back? On top of that, Anthony was acting nasty to me.

I stepped into the car and watched Anthony as he bopped his head to Tupac. Anthony only listened to him when he was trying to clear his mind. I sat in silence, staring out the window. My mind replayed the look in Jason's eyes before he sped away. I closed my eyes and filled my lungs with air and held it for as long as I could. Pushing the air out through my nose, I rubbed my legs and stretched.

I looked down at my phone and noticed a missed call. My old friends were waving to me in my stomach as I brushed the screen with my right thumb to look at the number. It was Jason. Pressing delete call, I glanced over at Anthony. He was busy singing along to the radio. I looked back down and swiped my screen with my thumb over the text messages icon. I gulped at the messages that were waiting.

I know you saw me

Who is that guy? I need to talk to you

I'll be here till Sunday. I love you. Call me back ASAP!

I looked out the corner of my eye to make sure Anthony was not looking at me. If he knew my ex-husband was calling and texting me, he would go off. If he knew that Jason had already text and called me before and that I didn't tell him, he'd be pissed.

I scrolled through social media sites and then clicked on my pictures icon and swiped through a few old pictures. I peeped over at Anthony just to make sure he wasn't watching me. Looking back down, I quickly switched over to my text messages and scrolled until I found Jason's messages.

The moment intensified as I kept one eye on Anthony and the other on my phone. I've watched teenagers on TV send messages in 2 seconds. This was my chance to see if I could do that, too.

My left hand rubbed up and down the side of the phone while my right hand did all the work. I had to make sure that Anthony didn't realize what I was doing. My heart beat hard through my chest as I quickly thumbed the message to Jason.

I don't know what you are doing here or what is going on, but don't try to start nothing with me. I will call you later on tonight.

I hit send and lay my phone down in my lap. I closed my eyes and turned my head toward the window. This was just too stressful.

I hated lying to Anthony. He was anal about being honest with each other. Keeping secrets from each other meant that you didn't respect the person you were with. And to Anthony, keeping secrets meant you were capable of doing anything behind his back. Even though I hadn't done anything wrong, this secret I was keeping from him was growing bigger by the moment.

I had to nip this issue in the bud right away before it became a pain in my side that I couldn't handle. I didn't want to worry about a thing. I had worried myself to death for five years while I was married and for two years after the divorce. Now that I had found someone whom I really love, there was no way I would be worried again.

Jason and I had some unfinished business to deal with. He obviously had something to prove. I had to get to the bottom of why he pulled this stunt, but not now. Not in front of Anthony and not until I had a clear head. I'll deal with it in the morning, I thought.

Anthony glanced over at me as we drove down the street. I forced a nervous smile at him, hoping he would return the favor. His teeth were white as snow, and his dark skin was glowing as he flashed that smile that I saw 25 years ago. My heart melted. I loved Anthony and I didn't want Jason to get in the way of my sanity and happiness. Anthony came with baggage that I didn't want to deal with. His insecurities from his ex-wife cheating on him were a big part of why he was always angry about people keeping secrets and telling lies. I wanted to make sure he trusted me.

Still holding my cell phone, I picked up my black leather purse on the floor and dropped it inside. I took my hand and placed it gently on Anthony's hand. Looking him in his eyes, I softly blew him a kiss. He softly squeezed my hand in reassurance and looked back at the road, still nodding his head. Tupac had eased his mind, for now.

For ten minutes we drove down the street. Anthony bopped his head and I sat in silence staring out the window. My purse, which lay on the floor next to my feet, was constantly vibrating on my leg. I ignored it. I knew I had to deal with Jason, but not today, not now.

Jason

Two days passed since I zoomed away from Andrea and Mr. Darkness. No calls and no text from her. The day I left her house, I pulled into the Renaissance Hotel parking garage and turned off the car. Taking a deep breath, I looked around to see if I was being followed. Except for a few cars parked in valet spots, the garage was empty and dark. I looked around again. No red car. No Andrea. No Mr. Darkness. I groaned.

When I drove away, it seemed like everyone in the neighborhood had seen me. I imagined Andrea screaming my name and driving around trying to find me. I imagined Mr. Darkness trying to figure out who I was.

I opened and closed my sweaty palms and rolled my eyes. I didn't know what I was expecting to happen when I pulled up next to Andrea, but just the thought of another man touching her made my skin crawl.

Sweat rolled down the back of my neck and stuck to my black linen shirt. I adjusted the collar and looked into the rearview mirror. No one was signaling for me. No one was yelling or cursing for me to get out of the car. I looked down on the floor in the back seat. A rumpled white T-shirt covered a tan baseball bat. I kept it with me whenever I decided to go for long walks in the neighborhood.

It had been ten minutes since I sent Andrea a text message and she hadn't responded. Maybe they were long gone, enjoying each other's company in that red car. Maybe she and Mr. Darkness were somewhere locking lips. The images of them together resurrected my anger. My jaw tightened as the sweat grew on my neck and eyebrows.

"Well, she knows I'm here and she knows I've seen her new boy toy. I guess I have no other choice but to wait for her to call me." I became angry. There was no way I would leave without talking or seeing her again. I didn't drive all this way for nothing.

I tapped my foot on the carpet. I hated waiting for an answer. I hated waiting for people to call me back. How disrespectful it was of her not to call me. The history we had was great. Sure we had bumps along the way, but what married couple didn't? I had to believe that there was a way for us to reconnect. She just needed to know that I was doing better. She needed to know that I had money now to take care of us both. She needed to know there was no other man for her.

Three hours passed with no call or text from Andrea. Defeat held my hand as I took the walk of shame back to my room. I took a quick shower and sat on bed, retracing my thoughts. Seconds later, my cell rang and vibrated on the nightstand.

Andrea was face timing me from her iPhone. I quickly took the towel from around my neck so that my chest would be exposed. She was beautiful. Her hair was pulled up in a bun, and her lips had a tint of red on them. *Sade* was playing in the background.

Her voice was raspy as if she'd been yelling and she had bags under her eyes.

"Hey."

"Well that's a hell of a welcome. Sorry to disappoint you."

She rubbed the tip of her nose and yawned. "Ok, Jason, you come here unannounced, racing around like you're a stunt man. What's going on, what are you trying to prove after all this time?"

I closed my eyes and exhaled. The lines in my forehead gathered together. Sweat formed around my forehead. "I don't know what to say. I missed you. I need you. I can't handle my character being assassinated anymore. I'm going crazy without you!"

I paused and looked for her to answer. She sat quietly. Confusion and concern spilled out of her eyes and onto her face. I inhaled and blew my breath out and tried again.

"I let you down."

She looked down. "You did."

Her head rose and a tear rolled down her left cheek. She wiped it away and stared at me.

I paused again. "Are you ok?"

I watched in silence as more tears flowed down her face.

"You know I'm not ok. Did you care four years ago when you walked out on me? Did you care when I had to pay two thousand dollars in rent by myself when you left? Did you care when I barely had enough food in the refrigerator, Jason?"

She wiped her eyes with her shirt sleeve and sighed. "This is too much for me, Jason. You deceived me for almost five years, walked out on me, and left me financially strapped, and then show up out of nowhere. How do you think I'm supposed to feel?"

I was as guilty as charged. I couldn't say anything. The words wouldn't come out. I was embarrassed. Seeing her hurt like that hurt me. I looked down as I spoke to her. I couldn't look at her eyes.

"I've fucked everything up. I know I was wrong. There is no way that I can apologize for what I did. There is nothing I can say to make things right. I've asked myself so many times how can I apologize for what I did? I don't know how to Andrea. I was in a bad way. I've been to counseling and I did a lot of soul searching. I want to make this right. I still love you, Andrea. Can we meet and talk in person?"

Andrea had a confused look on her face. Her mouth was open as if she was in shock. "Are you serious?"

"I'm doing really well now. I've got plenty of money. I can make sure we are ok now. I've gotten myself together."

She put her hands over her faced and groaned.

"Who's that guy that you were with, Andrea? Are you seeing him?"

"Does that even matter now, Jason? You lied to me. You left me hanging! She yelled. 'At least he doesn't lie to me like you did!"

Her words stung me and my tail was between my legs. "I can make this better, Andrea."

Her brown hair bounced gently off her shoulders as she shook her head. "No."

"Why not?"

"Because I said so, Jason. I got bills up my ass that need to be paid."

"I can take care of those bills, Andrea," I pleaded with her. "Come on. Meet with me one time, Andrea. Let's talk this out. We had some good times, right?"

She stared at me, pondering her next sentence. My words were reaching her.

"Please, Andrea. I can barely breathe without you. Just one meeting, and if you don't want to talk to me anymore after that, then I'll never call you again."

She took in a deep breath and blew it out long. She looked up at me and whispered, "I can't believe you are doing this now, Jason. Where were you when I had to borrow money from my family just to pay the past due bills you left behind?

Where was your concern when I had to ask my father to pay the house note for me because you didn't pay it before you left? Not one time have you called me to apologize for all the lies you told! What you got to say about that, Jason?"

"No matter what I say to you or to your family, Andrea, it wouldn't matter. I told you I was sorry and I meant it. I don't know what else to say. I was wrong. I wasn't in my right mind when everything started to happen. So I kept everything from you. I didn't know how to tell you we didn't have money for things. I know you liked to have nice things, and I was too embarrassed to say I didn't have any money."

The side of her lips poked out like a duck.

"When I lost my job, I was overwhelmed. And then we moved to the house I couldn't afford to pay for. I didn't know how to tell you."

"Wow," she said, looking away from the phone.

I moved the phone closer to my face so she could see how serious I was. Four years and I finally had a chance to tell my story to her. I had to make it good.

"I was lost. I've been lost, baby. It's like the life I wanted to give you turned into a fantasy." My voice cracked like a 13-year-old boy's. A lump formed in my throat. I coughed and swallowed hard. "I...I checked out, Andrea. The next thing I know I was smoking again and everything fell apart." I held my head down as tears rolled down my face.

Andrea put her fingers over her lips. "Am I supposed to believe you?" She cried for a minute and then wiped her face. I sat there frozen. This conversation was going completely left. This was not the reunion I had hoped for. "We are divorced, remember?"

I sucked my teeth. "You don't need to remind me, Andrea. I got the papers."

"Don't get an attitude, Jason. You brought this on yourself!"

"I need you right now, Andrea, and this is how you treat me?"

"Really? Fuck the way you feel. That is nothing compared to what I felt these last few years!"

"Well looking at the way you were kissing that guy, it didn't look like you were feeling bad at all. Who the fuck is he anyway, huh? Were you cheating on me when we were married?"

I snapped. This was the first time we ever yelled at each other. When we were married, we never yelled at each other. I guess we kept everything bottled up.

"You got some nerve, Jason. Maybe you should go cry on your mother's tits since she was always the third person in our relationship anyway."

"Fuck you the way you are fucking that dark ass guy." Heat rose from my neck. I was so pissed at her. This conversation was at its breaking point.

"Good, I'll go and do that now. How about I bring him in the room and suck his dick right in front of you then?" Her words had so much hate in them that they hit me with a pound of guilt.

I threw my phone against the wall. I was tired of going back and forth with her like Ike and Tina. I was beyond upset. I was mad at myself for talking to her that way. I couldn't believe she was talking to me the way she did. So many feelings ran through my head, and I didn't know what to do next.

I pushed myself back up on the bed and pulled a pillow from under the covers, tucking it under my neck.

I closed my eyes and saw her tears. I saw the anger she had for me. She was a broken woman. I created that broken woman.

My phone rang. I looked over on the floor and saw her face pop up again. She was face timing me.

I answered, "Yeah?"

"Look, I'm sorry I was vulgar. That wasn't me. I was so mad at you for what you did, and this anger has been built up for so long, so I'm saying I'm sorry." Her face was free from tears. She was calm.

"That's ok, I understand. I'm sorry, too. I didn't mean any of what I said. I do love you. I want you to understand that. I never meant to hurt you."

"I did love you when we were married. If I didn't, I would have run you over with my car." She let out a soft chuckle.

"Let's start over, Andrea. Can we meet for breakfast tomorrow?"

"I don't know, Jason, I'm seeing someone now. I don't want to mess up what we have. He's a nice guy. He doesn't even know I'm talking to you right now. I really love him, too." She looked away from the phone.

"Andrea, I can buy anything and everything I need and want right now. I just need some time with you. Just give me a few hours."

I'll give you one meeting. I guess I can do it after those messages you left me."

I smiled at her. "That's perfect."

"Look, I gotta go now, Jason."

"Where do you want to meet?" I smiled again showing more teeth.

"I don't know, how about Pancake House for breakfast tomorrow?" She flashed me a crooked smile.

Wow, I thought. This is really going to happen. She knows I love pancakes! Maybe this is a sign!

"Ok I'll see you at ten in the morning. Love you!" I flashed a peace sign.

She raised one eyebrow and made duck lips with her mouth again. "Don't push it, Jason. Bye."

The phone went black. I sat back on the bed and smiled. "Phew!" I fell back on the bed and sighed. The call drained me. I rubbed my head. My plan has worked, I thought. Now I have to convince Andrea that we should be back together. I had won half the battle. The next battle was to get rid of Mr. Darkness. I closed my eyes and made mental notes.

Get Andrea to talk to me. Check.

Get rid of Mr. Darkness. Next.

Anthony

The house was dark and quiet when I walked in. That's odd, I thought. Andrea normally waits up for me before going to sleep. Our dinner conversation was long and quiet. Besides looking down at her phone every few minutes, Andrea was nervous and hardly talked to me. No matter what I said to her, she wasn't all there. After dinner, I dropped her off at home and then stopped over a friend's house to talk about our new workout video.

I walked up the stairs to see if she was sleeping. The hallway was dark except for a dim light underneath the closed bedroom door.

"She must have left the TV on," I said as I tiptoed toward the door. Andrea always fell asleep with the TV on so I was not surprised. I was just about to reach my hand out and turn the knob when I heard voices coming from the other side of the door.

Confusion was written all over my face when the voice was a deeper tone than hers.

"Who in the hell is she talking to?" Quietly, I pressed my head up against the door. I could hear my heart beat through my chest as my right eye squinted to hear the soft conversation. I've never been one to eavesdrop on someone else's phone call, but my feet wouldn't allow me to turn around and walk away.

My eyes widened with shock as I listened to Andrea talk to the unknown man. My jaw dropped as I blacked out. All I remember was someone saying, "I love you, Andrea." At that very moment I was a lion waiting to pounce on the zebra. I wanted to open the door and catch her in the act of talking to another man. I wanted to see the horror on her face when I grabbed the phone from her and screamed at the person on the other line. My stomach ached with disappointment. How could she cheat on me? All the love I had for her drained from my face and down to my feet as I stood there in silence.

I didn't know what to do. My mind told me to sit down in front of the door to catch my breath, but a part of me told me to wait.

When my ex-wife cheated on me, life as I knew it was over. I've always had trust issues, but when Andrea came along, she changed all of that. She was my saving grace, my best friend. Just the thought of her cheating on me put me into a rage.

With my pride laying on the floor and my head hung low, I walked downstairs and sat on the living room sofa. Defeat filled my heart. My eyes were blurry as hot tears rolled down my face. I became angry as I realized my trust had been broken. Within ten minutes, the woman I adored had become the woman I hated.

I took a deep breath in and held it. As I blew it out hard, my teeth clenched and my fists balled tightly into circles. "Do you think you're going to sneak around on me and get away with it? Oh baby, you have met your match!" I stood and pounded my fists together. "So you gonna meet tomorrow at the Pancake House, huh? Well guess I'll be the surprise entree then."

I grabbed my keys off the sofa and walked out, slamming the front door behind me.

As I walked to my car, the unknown man's voice echoed through my head: *I love you, Andrea...I love you, Andrea.*

"Damn!" I stumbled back as I kicked the side of the car door, leaving a scratch. "Damn you, Andrea! All the love I gave you and this is how you treat me?"

The corvette took the curves smoothly as I shifted the gears from one to two. I had nowhere to go, so I just drove. The voices I heard played over and over in my mind, resurrecting more anger. My jaws were tight, and my heart trotted like a horse.

Seconds later, my cell beeped. It was Andrea. I cursed and pressed ignore. She dialed my goddamn number, and I felt violated.

The phone rang again. I didn't want to talk to her, but I had to hear what she wanted from me and why she was calling me.

"What!" I spat out.

"Were you just here? Why did you leave?" she said softly.

"Andrea, don't play with me, you know I was there. What do you want?"

"Are you mad that I went to bed early? I was tired, I'm sorry."

"Really, Andrea? That's all you have to say?" Either she was playing stupid or I was dreaming. Either way, I was not in the mood to be the mouse.

"What did I do, Anthony? Damn. Every time I turn around, you are mad about something, geez!"

I decided to play her game. "So what were you doing before you went to sleep, Andrea?"

I sat and listened to her soft breathing. She was quiet.

My tone became rough. "Did you hear me?"

"Does it matter? You were out with your friends. But if you need to know, I took a bath and then went to sleep."

My blood was boiling. Not only was she talking to another man behind my back, but she was lying like I didn't mean anything to her.

"Not true. Anyway, do you wanna go to breakfast in the morning?" I eagerly waited for her answer.

"No, I have to meet my friend Rhonda for breakfast to talk about our work event in the morning."

"Who? Since when? You never said anything to me about it today when we were out."

"Stop trippin', Anthony. You plan plenty of things and forget to tell me."

My heart broke into a billion pieces. I accepted my defeat and waved the white flag.

"Ok then, well, I'll call you after your meeting, Andrea."

"Ok, love you." Her voice trailed off and the call ended just as fast as it started.

It was time to get this over with. I knew what I had to do, and I had always hoped I'd never have to do this. Visions of Andrea with another man made my skin crawl. I cringed at how easy it was for her to lie to me like we had no history together. Twenty-five years of love that I carried for this woman was sliding down the drain. I scowled and pulled my car into the driveway of my house.

Hours went by as I sat in the car plotting what I would do. Birds were slowly singing me songs of a new day as the moonlight moved behind the sun. Before I knew it, it was six in the morning. I rubbed my eyes and blinked hard. I couldn't believe I allowed someone to take over my mind like this.

I knew what I had to do. I needed to see this man who was proclaiming his love for my woman. I wanted to see the man who Andrea decided was worth lying to me about. "I hope he is worth it, Andrea."

I was being faced with the reality that my relationship with Andrea was about to become non-existent. But in that moment, I wasn't ready to accept the fact that I had allowed someone to control my heart. She had lied to me. She had cheated on me, I thought. The power of love was leaking out of my veins with the speed of light. I was tired of being hurt by women. No matter how hard I loved them, the pain they put on me was worse. Unfortunately, Andrea was added to the list of people who had hurt me. I was bombarded by a million thoughts, each one pressed against my brain like an aneurysm. I had to release this pain, but my mind wouldn't let me.

So there I sat, in silence, waiting for something to happen. I waited for Andrea to call me back to tell me everything was going to be ok. Hoping that if I blinked hard enough, I'd realize that this was just a dream and I'd walk back to Andrea's house and lay next to her.

I opened my eyes and looked down at my shirt. The sweat on my chest had started to dry up and stick to my white shirt. I raised my hands and grabbed the steering wheel and put the car into reverse. Like a broken record, the voice continued to play over and over again in my head: *I love you...I love you.* My jaws clenched so tight my lips were sore.

The voice rang through my head so long that I when looked up I was pulling into the parking lot of the Pancake House. I had no idea what I was going to do. I had no idea what I was going to say to her. I sat next to the building so I wouldn't be seen. I wanted to see her pull up. I wanted to see whom she was there to meet. I was ready to face the music. I hope Andrea was, too.

Andrea

The bags under my eyes were just as heavy as the guilt that was swirling around in my head as I sat in the parking lot of the Pancake House waiting for Jason to arrive. Doubt sat in the passenger next to me as I contemplated leaving and going back home. Why did I agree to meet with him? Maybe I still had some leftover feelings for my ex-husband. Maybe I needed to get closure. I didn't know the real story as to why he was financially messed up. I never found out why he was never able to pay our bills on time.

Anthony's face flashed in front of my eyes. He was the man of my dreams. He was the man I loved. He was the man who walked into my life when I was down on my luck and put a smile to my face. And he was the man who never lied to me. Running my fingers through my hair, I thought about Anthony and how I had lied to him. If I would have just told him from day one that Jason was contacting me, I wouldn't be sitting in this parking lot waiting on my ex-husband. I shook my head in disbelief. I looked out the window and mumbled, "Every time I turn around, something about Jason pops up. If it's not one thing, it's another.

"I'll just go in here, see what Jason wants, and then get back to my life with Anthony." I looked down at my cell phone. He was late. I blew my breath and looked behind me. How is he gonna worry me to death to meet him and then he shows up late? Maybe Jason's lateness was a good thing. I didn't need to be here anyway. If Anthony knew I was here to see my ex-husband, he'd kill me. I could just leave and go back home and act like nothing ever happened.

"Yeah, I'll just do that. I'll leave, tell him I couldn't wait any longer, and he'll leave and go back to where he came from."

Just as I reached to turn the key in the ignition, a gold Cadillac flew past me and slammed on its brakes in the parking space in front of me. Startled, I jumped in my seat, whipping my hair around. Jason waved, offering me a devilish grin. He looked like the happiest person on earth.

I scowled at him and jumped out the car. "Did you need to make an appearance like that? And you are late." I frowned at him.

"Sorry, babes, I overslept," he said, walking out of the car with his arms stretched out to hug me.

I blocked his hands with my arms. "Don't try it. Let's just go in." I was not in the mood for hugs. I didn't know why he was so cheerful, especially after all this time of being apart from each other. I just wanted to get this over with and figure out how I was going to deal with Anthony.

"Oh yeah, I forgot you are not a morning person." He chuckled as he walked ahead of me to open the door.

I watched him as he glided to the door. He looked different. He wasn't the same person who walked out on me years ago. He was happier. A healthier body now replaced the frail piece of a man he used to be. His skin was clear. The scraggly hairs that once covered his mouth and chin was now a lined up goatee trimmed to perfection. Jeans that barely hung on his waist was now replaced with a pair of black fitted Armani slacks. Stacey Adams black shoes graced his feet. His white Sean Jean button down shirt had a hint of cologne that lingered in the air. My lungs filled with the soft smell of his scent, and I almost smiled with approval. He looked good, and I definitely noticed.

The restaurant was pretty empty except for a few senior citizens who were sipping their morning brew.

"Let's sit there." I pointed to a small booth for two in the back corner. I didn't want anyone to hear our conversation, and I also wanted to make sure that no one recognized me. The last thing I needed was for someone to see me having breakfast with my ex-husband. The streets would be filled with gossip.

I could feel his eyes covering my body as I looked around for the waitress. I tried my best to avoid eye contact with him. I didn't want any added attention.

"You look good, Andrea. How are you?"

I found my eyes moving from his eyes to his lips. They were not as dark as they were the last time I saw him. He must have stopped smoking, I thought.

"How do you think I am, Jason? I've been in financial debt since you left me. That's how I'm doing." My words were soft, but cold.

"I know I left you in shambles, but that's why I'm here. I'm making a good living for myself, and I want to make things right between us."

My eyes widened at his words, and they caught my attention. If he was going to help me get out of debt, I was all ready to listen to him. I didn't want him to think I was excited about his money, so I kept a straight face.

I placed both of my elbows on the table. "Oh, is that right?" My knuckles covered my mouth while the palm of my hand cupped my chin. "And paying my bills is supposed to fix five years of lies, Jason? You hurt me, and you put my family in financial situations because they had to help me, Jason. You did a lot."

My words stung him, and his smile was replaced with concern. "Look, I know I hurt you. I know I was not the husband you were supposed to marry. I didn't communicate with you like I should have. I wanted to tell you from the beginning that I didn't have the money, but I was ashamed.

"I never wanted to hurt you. You don't know how much I have beat myself up for the lies I told. I've been a mess ever since, Andrea."

My heart softened as I looked into his eyes. He was genuine. When we were married, I was always able to tell he was lying to me. But this time, the truth was written all over his face.

For years, I looked for closure in the death of my marriage. I had even forgiven him for what he had done to me just so I could move on. I never thought I'd be hearing an apology from him after all this time.

The ceiling fan blew traces of his cologne into my nose. I closed my eyes and inhaled deep. Forgiveness was on the tip of my tongue, but I wasn't ready to release it. Not just yet. The elephant was not only in the room, but he was running across my mind like a stampede.

"Jason, this is just too much. I forgave you for what you did to me, but the pain is still there. I would have done anything to make sure we were ok financially. All you had to do was just tell me, and I would have made it happen." I spilled years of hurt onto the table.

And he slid out of the booth, stood up, and wiped his face.

Confused, I looked up at him *He's leaving?* I thought.

Just then, he walked over and sat next to me. I scooted over and held my breath. With his arm wrapped around my shoulder, he wept. Tears flowed down his cheek. I didn't know what to do, so I rocked from side to side.

"It's ok, Jason. It's over. I forgive you. It's in the past now. I'm not holding any grudges."

He wiped his face with a napkin sitting on the table.

"I never wanted this to happen. I love you, Andrea.

I just want you to forgive me. Please forgive me."

And at that moment, I saw something that I never saw before. He was vulnerable. His unbreakable heart was open and ready to bond with my broken heart.

"We'll figure it out, Jason." I laid my head on his shoulder. We sat there in silence. I exhaled and we bonded.

"I can't say that we will get back together, Jason, because too much time has passed." I took another breath, and he looked up at me. "But we can start off by being friends. For now, that's all I can say."

Jason sniffed and slowly smiled. "Ok. Now where's that damn waitress, I'm hungry!"

We laughed together. That hadn't happened in years.

Anthony

The pain in my chest was so hard that I fell against the door. I fought back the anger as I watched the two of them embrace. At first I didn't know who the man was sitting with her in the booth, but then I remembered a picture of him in her bedroom drawer. It was Andrea's ex-husband Jason. And then it all hit me at once. Everything made sense. The weird way she was acting when I saw her throw her cell phone under her pillow. I felt her hesitation when I tried to kiss her as we lay in the bed. The distraction that took over her body when the gold car sped away from us outside of her house just before we were to go out on a date.

The same gold car was sitting in the parking lot of the Pancake House the morning after I heard another man tell her he loved her.

Part of my mind told me to leave and talk to Andrea at home, but the other part took me to another level of anger. I had an out of body experience as I approached their table. Everything went black. Heat rose from my neck like fire and my chest rose up and down like the incredible hulk as I stood in front of them. My eyesight was blurry as I balled up my right fist. The muscles in my arms tensed up with so much power that I couldn't control the intensity of its movement. My fist moved past Andrea's face like the matrix and landed right on his mouth.

The blow to his face muffled her screams. Andrea held on to the wooden chair next to the table with fear scrolling across her face. My eyes met hers as we watched him lay on the floor, holding his bloody lip. My breathing was fast. It took minutes for me to calm down and realize what I had just done.

"How could you cheat on me, Andrea? I've been here this whole time while this nigga been who knows where living the good life. You meeting niggas behind my back? You call this love?" Evil spat out of my mouth and surrounded her like the grim reaper. She stood there crying while he laid there mumbling.

"Anthony! Please! You've got it all wrong," she said. "Nothing happened, you have it all wrong. It's not what you think!"

"It's not what I think? I think my woman is fucking another man. That's what I think!"

Andrea lost her balance as she reached out to grab my arm. I pulled back and stood over Jason.

I wanted to beat his ass. I wanted to put him in a hospital. I stood there breathing over him, both my fists balled up, ready to pounce on him like a lion. Sweat dripped off my forehead and landed on his head. He trembled.

Elderly customers stood around in shock as they waited for the next scene to play out. I paused and flashed them a '*don't you dare say a word*' look.

Tears mixed with black mascara ran down Andrea's cheekbones. Her breathing was rough.

"Anthony," she whimpered, "stop, don't do it. He's already hurt."

"I'm fucking done with you." Disgust filled my face as I watched her. "If that is what you want, then you can have him!" I turned around and raised my leg up to step over Jason's limp body and stormed out of the restaurant.

I drove out of the parking lot like I had left a crime scene. My heart ached. Blood dripped from my knuckles. Andrea fucked me over, and I was ashamed that I got caught up in her fake love.

It took me a minute to realize this situation was far from over. Before I knew it, I was speeding back to the restaurant. There was business that needed to be finished.

Andrea was holding Jason as they walked out the door. Concern etched her face as she walked him to his car. She hadn't noticed that I was sitting there watching them. Just like she didn't know I watched her from the window putting her head on his goddamn shoulder.

I ran my teeth over my gums and sucked my teeth. I couldn't believe that I had fallen in love with this woman.

I opened up my glove compartment and stared at the silver beauty inside. I ran my fingertips over her. My eyes squinted. I grabbed my .38 and made sure it was loaded. My body was filled with so much rage. *I love you, Andrea* echoed in my head. I grabbed my temples and screamed. "Shut up!" I took a deep breath and pointed my hand toward Andrea. It was time to teach her a lesson. No one would ever hurt me again.

As she closed the driver side door, Andrea glanced back and saw me standing there. Horror filled her eyes.

She made a sound that I had never heard before. "Anthony! No!" She turned to run toward me in a panic.

Voices in my head spoke louder than I had ever heard before. *If you take her back, she'll hurt you again.* The force of the bullet exiting the gun pushed my hand back on the car door. My breathing was heavy as I shook my head. I did what I had to do. I didn't want to be known as the man who killed his girlfriend for cheating, but I had to send a message.

Everything was silent. It went so fast. I paused and looked up.

Andrea lay on the ground. Jason peeped over his steering wheel frozen in place. I didn't run, but I wanted to. My feet drug across the gravel as I walked over to her. Her breathing was ragged. She was terrified. Her hair was dirty from the gravel that covered her face. She looked up at me like a frightened baby.

"I should kill you." I looked at her in disgust. "I tried to love you. You are lucky all I did was shoot in the air." She took a deep breath and trembled. "Don't you ever call me again. I'm done with you." I turned and walked back to my car, making no eye contact with Jason. He was still peeping over the steering wheel.

I drove off, racing my engine and leaving Andrea in a cloud of smoke. I was a jealous man. I could've shot and killed them both. But I didn't. All she had to do was tell me she didn't want to be with me anymore. I exhaled and swallowed. I looked over in the passenger seat, my gun resting after its day out.

I've never lied to anyone. I never had a reason to. Andrea knew that. I played our relationship over and over again. What did I do for her to lie to me? Was I too soft? I'd never know. What causes someone to lie when they can tell the truth and deal with the consequences? Life would be so much easier. Andrea had begged and borrowed to get out of debt. I couldn't believe she allowed this man to come back into her life. I thought we had a good life together. I thought she was the woman for me. After all this time, all this love that I gave, I was left with nothing.

I couldn't go home, and I damn sure couldn't go back to Andrea's house. The streets were hot and my name was probably written all over them. It was too hot for me to stay here in Texas. I had to get away where no one could find me.

I reached into my pocket and pulled out my cell phone. I scrolled down my contact list and stopped on a name. I couldn't trust this person, but I knew she would have my back if need be.

Blood stains sat on my knuckles as I pressed my ear against the phone, waiting for her to answer.

"Anthony? Is that you?"

"Hey Janet, I need to come to your house right now, is that cool?"

"Umm...sure. All the way here in Washington State?"

"Yep." I took a breath. "I'm going to catch a flight, and I'll be there in five hours."

She was shocked and happy at the same time. "Ok! Text me when you get in, and I'll pick you up from the airport."

"Cool." I took a breath and hung up the phone. Even though Janet, my ex-wife, cheated on me years ago, we only talked a few times a year when I called her to check in on our son whom I left behind when we divorced. I never told Andrea about my son. I just didn't think she needed to know right away. Plus she had her own lies she was hiding from me so it didn't matter. Janet had always wanted to get back with me. I hated her for cheating on me, but when she told me she was pregnant with my son, I hated her a little less. I couldn't stand her at times, but maybe Andrea cheating on me was a sign. Whatever the sign was, I'd have to deal with it another time.

Today was a new day and the end of Andrea and Anthony.